T0132382

LIN. WOODS

SEE ME
not my
COLOR:

ANOTHER KENNY CAN LIFE
LESSON STORY

To order additional copies of this book, contact:
Xlibris
844-714-8691
www.Xlibris.com
Orders@Xlibris.com

ISBN: Softcover   978-1-6698-5980-2
         EBook   978-1-6698-5979-6

Print information available on the last page

Rev. date: 12/20/2022

SEE ME
not my
COLOR:
ANOTHER KENNY CAN LIFE LESSON STORY

"Man-oh-man! It's Saturday morning, my favorite day of the week! I don't have to go to school. I don't have to go to church. But I know one thing for sure, I am going to the park!" said Kenny Can at the top of his lungs.

Kenny sprang out of bed like a frog jumping from a lily pad, ran to the window and let the sun fill the room and bounce off his co-co brown skin. His bright smile went from ear to ear at just the thought of spending all day Saturday in his favorite place in the whole wide world, Inspired Park.

Next, Kenny rushed to the bathroom, washed his face and hands, and brushed his teeth until they shined a spectacular pearly white. "You are one cool dude," Kenny said to himself as he looked in the bathroom mirror. Then he sang loudly, "Kenny Can, Yes you can, Yes you can, You u know you can, Yes you can, Kenny Can!"

"Please stop all of that noise!" Kenny's big sister Lisa said loudly. "I'm trying to get some sleep!"

"Sorry Lisa," said Kenny as he finished dressing. He put on his favorite pair of jeans, his *Yes You Can Kenny* Can white T-shirt and favorite pair of white sneakers. "Me and my crew are going to Inspired Park! I am so thankful today is such a beautiful sunny day!"

Kenny grabbed his cell phone and started a group chat with his crew, his cousins Lori, Mike-Mike and Trey-Trey.

Kenny: Man-oh-Man, it's great you all are here. Let's meet at my house and walk to Inspired Park. We can play, get on the swings, shoot some hoops and hang out all day!

Lori: Awesome! Sounds like a plan. Can't wait to see you guys. Family togetherness!
I love it!

Mike-Mike: You know I'm there dude.

Trey-Trey: Obviously! I am coming too cuzzos!

Kenny: Alright then. I'll see you here in 30 minutes.

Lori: Why 30 minutes? It is not going to take you that long to get ready.

Kenny: Girl, I have to do my morning routine which includes my positive affirmations, listen to my favorite songs, wash up, get dressed, put on my smell good stuff.

You know how I do! And I need my big boy strength to deal with you!

Trey-Trey: Word!

Mike-Mike: I love it! See you soon Kenny.

Lori: Bye!

Trey-Trey: I'm out!

Kenny: I'm glad we all live in the same neighborhood. I love my family!

All of a sudden Kenny smelled a delicious aroma floating up from the kitchen to his bedroom. "Mom is that my favorite food in the whole wide world you are cooking!" yelled Kenny.

"If you mean banana pancakes, then yes," said mom. Kenny ran down the steps and rushed to the kitchen table. He let out a loud, "Man, oh man!" and began gobbling down the pancakes quicker than you an count to five.

As Kenny took his last bite of banana pancake, the doorbell rang. He raced to the door, flung it wide open, and there were his three favorite cousins, Lori, Mike-Mike and Trey-Trey. Kenny said, "What's up cuzzos?"

Lori said, "Good to see you little cuz." Kenny snapped back, "What do you mean *little* cuz? I'm just as big as you." Lori hit him back up with, "In your dreams Kenny Can. I'm a whole two inches taller than you." "Whatever man. You know I love you girl," Kenny replied.

Mike-Mike shook his head, looked at the both of them and said, "Are you two going to waste time with this back-and-forth stuff or are we going to the park for some fun? Let's go!"

Trey chimed in, "Ditto!"

Kenny waved good-bye to his mom and said, "We're out." He and his cousins began the ten-minute trip to Inspired Park. They locked arms and started singing as they walked.

Lori looked at Kenny and said in a smart-mouthed tone, "Don't you mean, let's start walking instead of we're out?" Kenny was getting a little irritated with her and cut his eyes at her. Lori decided then to sing a togetherness song to make everyone smile, "I Got You. You got me. And God's got us all...can't you see?"

Kenny looked up to the sky and said, "Please help her because she cannot sing!" The boys laughed. Lori gave Kenny that *boy, I am not playing with you* look but smiled when Kenny looked away. The foursome grinned at each other and continued walking, talking, singing, and laughing on their way.

And just like that, they arrived at their favorite place in the city, Inspired Park.

The temperature was just right for some fun in the park. The crew started running towards one of their favorite spots at the park, the big bright yellow swings. Kenny looked around and noticed there were people everywhere, on the bike trail, the jogging path, under the trees, around the lake, the merry-go-round, the giant wheel and almost everywhere in between.

Kenny looked around the park trying to find the perfect hang-out space. He looked to the north, south, east and west and said, "Man-oh-man! The park is s-o-o-o-o packed today. I mean look at the swings, and my favorite, the monkey bars! There is a long line for everything that I love. Looks like we'll be waiting until Jesus comes!"

Lori snapped her fingers and said in a matter-of-fact way, "No worries, Kenny, I'll just tell God to move the line along with a quickness and we will be on those swings before you know it."

The crew stood by a tree. They waited, and waited. After about fifteen minutes Kenny said, "I guess God's busy. Huh Lori?"

Just then Kenny heard someone calling his name. "Kenny Can! Kenny Can!"

It was his best friend Jake waiving at him from a few feet away. Kenny could pick Jake out from any crowd with his fiery red hair, green eyes and face dotted with brown freckles and a bold personality to match.

"Man oh Man, it's my boy Jake!" yelled Kenny. "I know I'm about to have big-fun now! What's up Jake?" Jake smiled through his shiny braces and said, "I'm here at the park with my mom. I didn't know you'd be here. But this is so cool!"

"For sure!" said Kenny. "And these are my cousins Lori, Mike-Mike and Trey-Trey. And cuzzos, I know you remember my brother from another mother, Jake." Lori smiled and said, "Coolness!" Mike-Mike agreed, "Yep." Trey-Trey answered with his usual, "Obviously!"

Now all five stood in line together waiting to get on the swings, the monkey bars or whatever opened up first. Just then a tall, blonde haired boy from Kenny and Jake's school named Evan walked right past Kenny, Trey-Trey, Lori and Mike-Mike without saying hello or excuse me, and spoke only to Jake, "Hey Jake. What's up?"

Jake said to Evan. "I'm good. But why are you with this chocolate crew? Come with me and I'll get us on the swings or monkey bars in a snap," said Evan.

"What about my friends?" asked Jake. "I'm not trying to mix all those colors in my milkshake. I like to keep it vanilla. You feel me?" said Evan

Kenny, Lori, Mike-Mike and Trey-Trey all stood frozen with their eyes wide open and their mouths open even wider. "Man-oh-Man! I can't believe he said what I thought I heard him say," said Kenny.

Jake looked at the crew. He felt bad and sad all at the same time. He could not believe his friend Evan could say such hurtful things. He took a deep breath, counted to ten and said to Evan, "I thought you were cool. But what you just said was not cool at all. So, you don't want to hang out with my friends because their skin color is a different?

My mom and dad taught me that people are people. It doesn't matter if they are red, blue, yellow, brown, black or white. It's only skin color. And you should not judge a person because of the way the look. We are all the same on the inside. How would you like it if I said I could not play with you because you have blonde hair and blue eyes?" All of a sudden Evan's face turned as white as snow. He said, "What? I don't get it."

Kenny jumped in, "Or what if we told you, you couldn't hang with us because you don't have soul-power like the chocolate ranger?"

"Yeah, we are all a part of one big family and one race, the human race. Your color does not matter. We should treat each other with love and respect," said Lori.

Mike-Mike said, "Ditto." Trey-Trey smiled from ear to ear and said, "Obviously!"

After that, Evan felt really bad about what he'd said to Kenny Can and his cousins. Love had moved his heart. He looked at everyone and said, "You guys are right. Color should not matter. People are people, no matter if they are purple green or blue! And besides, I see now that you guys are really cool, peeps."

Kenny said, "So Evan, the next time you see me, See Me, not my color!"

Jake said, "Amen brother!" Lori added, "And a hallelujah on top of that!" Mike-Mike agreed, "Double-ditto!" Trey-Trey said, "Obviously!"

Kenny Can's heart felt warm and fuzzy inside. He looked at everyone and said, "Just another beautiful Saturday at the park with family, my best friend Jake and my new friend Evan."

The End

SEE ME NOT MY COLOR: ANOTHER KENNY CAN LIFE LESSON STORY

BY LIN. WOODS

Life Lesson Questions For You

What lesson did you get from this story?

_____

Besides helping Evan to see the crew for who they are and not their color. What other life lesson did Kenny Can show toward Evan?

Answer: (forgiveness)

Have you ever met someone and judged them because of how they look before getting to know them?

_____

If you were Kenny Can, how would you have handled the situation with Evan?

_____

SEE ME NOT MY COLOR: ANOTHER KENNY CAN LIFE LESSON STORY

By LIN. WOODS

See Me Not My Color: Another Kenny Can Life Lesson Story is the story of the young boy Kenny Can who encounters racism on an otherwise beautiful day in the park with family and friends. A schoolmate initially judges Kenny Can and his cousins by the color of their skin and not their character. That is until he sees past their color to find new friends.

See Me No My Color: Another Kenny Can Life Lesson Story is dedicated to the memory of Kendrick I. Woods, the author's nephew. He lost his life at age 19 to senseless gun violence in 2017.

Printed in the United States
by Baker & Taylor Publisher Services